The Case of The Giggles

Written by Karen M. Bobos
Illustrated by Brittany Roberson

Please visit BobosBabes.com

Published by PlayPen Publishing
PlayPenPublishing.com

ISBN: 978-1-7343610-9-4 Paperback Edition

ISBN: 978-1-7343610-8-7 Hardback Edition

United States

Dedication

To my daughters -- my muses, my inspirations, my why --
Who gave me the courage to find my passion that I tucked aside.
May their love for each other and their passion for life
Help you find your own Angel, Princess, and Fairy inside.

The three little Bobos Babes, who lived in a magical land,
Shared a bond of love and loyalty that only close sisters could understand.

Scarlett was a delicate angel; her skin had heavenly powers.
Her touch could turn a barren land into a field of fragrant flowers.

Cora, the fairy, was as quick as lightening and the smallest of the three sisters.
She was blessed with enchanted hearing and could hear the quietest whispers.

Daphne, a beautiful princess, was a very silly and curious middle child.
She loved making her sisters laugh and charming them with her style.

She possessed the power to see the best in every situation they faced.
"Love never fails when happiness is the goal," was the motto she embraced.

Every morning the Babes ate their breakfast in the highest of their castle's towers.
They loved overlooking the land, enjoying the sunshine and occasional showers.

One morning, Princess Daphne hiccuped, followed by a sneeze and a laugh.
The Babes laughed along at her sounds and said their usual, "Oh Daph!"

As the girls continued to eat their bananas and berries and cream,
They noticed Princess Daphne's laugh was getting louder, like a scream.

"Oh no," said Angel Scarlett, "Princess Daphne has a case of the giggles."
She continued, "I saw it happen once before to our friend, Mr. Wiggles."

"Her laugh is so loud," said Fairy Cora. "It's hurting my tiny ears."
The Babes tried to make her laugh stop with their magical cheers.

"1, 2, 3, BOBOS BABES!" they shouted, but no such luck; her laughter did not rest.
Angel Scarlett said, "It's time to find someone who would know what is best."

The Bobos Babes whistled for Luke, their giant dog, whom they loved so dear.
They hopped up on his back, nestled into his fur, and said, "Hurry to the pier!"

Luke galloped across the land with the Babes holding onto his collar tight.
Within moments, they reached the pier, where Mr. Wiggles was in sight.

"Mr. Wiggles! Mr. Wiggles!" Angel Scarlett shouted with delight.
"We need your help, please! We need your personal insight!"

"Me?" said Mr. Wiggles, a worm that lived a quiet life.
"No one ever needs my help," he said, "not even my wife."

"We need your help," said Fairy Cora. "Oh please, Mr. Wiggles!
Princess Daphne has what you had … a case of the giggles."

"A case of the giggles?" he asked. "That sure was a terrible time I once had.
Who would have known that so much laughing could make someone so sad?"

"Oh, Mr. Wiggles," said Angel Scarlett. "What did you do to make it stop?"
"Well, I … umm …" Mr. Wiggles tried to remember. "Oh no! I forgot."

Mr. Wiggles tried to remember but said, "I just cannot recall what I did."
Looking at Princess Daphne he said, "Gee, I forgot. I'm so sorry, kid."

"Oh no, Mr. Wiggles," said Angel Scarlett. "If a memory comes back to you,
If you remember what stopped your giggles, or recall even a clue …

Simply shout out, 'Bobos Babes!'" continued Angel Scarlett, "and we'll head back.
Now we must go find another friend to help with this code we cannot crack."

The Babes traveled across the land and reached the den of Leonard the Lion.
He was the wisest animal in the land; he solved problems without even trying.

"Leonard the Lion!" shouted Fairy Cora. "We need your help, please!
Princess Daphne cannot stop laughing, and it all started with a sneeze."

"I wish that I could help," he said, "but I'm not the type of animal who giggles.
I know this happened once before to the worm by the pier, Mr. Wiggles."

He continued, "My laugh is a bit different. I'm more of a "ha ha" kind of guy.
I don't have a single giggle bone in me," Leonard the Lion said with a sigh.

"We already asked Mr. Wiggles," said Angel Scarlett, "but he cannot recall.
He tried to think of how he stopped it, but he had no memory of it at all."

"Ask Barbara the Butterfly," Leonard said. "She is the happiest friend I know.
She is always gracious and kind and brings joy wherever she may go.

She must know about laughter and all that it entails.
I bet she can solve your dilemma. She never fails!"

The Babes rushed off to see Barbara the Butterfly at her home
Amidst a field of flowers that Angel Scarlett helped her grow.

She was fluttering around the carnations, her favorite flower in her field.
"Barbara!" the Babes shouted. "We need whatever help that you can yield!"

"What's the matter, Bobos Babes?" the Butterfly said. "How can I assist?"
Barbara the Butterfly fluttered her wings and blew the Bobos Babes a kiss.

"Princess Daphne has the giggles," said Angel Scarlett. "It started this morning.
She had a hiccup and a sneeze, and then the giggles came with no warning."

"Oh dear," said Barbara the Butterfly, "that sounds like a pickle!
I had a friend that happened to. It started with a tickle."

"Actually," continued Barbara the Butterfly, "it started with his wife.
She thought laughter was just the answer to bring a little spice to his life.

His name is Mr. Wiggles. He is a worm living near the pier.
He's kind of a quiet guy. His wife wanted him to feel cheer."

"We know Mr. Wiggles, but when we asked him, he could not put a finger,"
Said Fairy Cora, "on what made his laughter continue to linger and linger."

"His laughter finally stopped," said Barbara the Butterfly.
"When his wife gave him a big hug and winked her eye."

The Babes grabbed their laughing sister and hugged her with all their might.
They winked both eyes together; they winked eye left and winked eye right!

Then all of a sudden, the laughing had ceased.
"Oh," said Princess Daphne, "I am oh so pleased."

"I really love laughing," said Daphne. "It is one of my favorite things,"
She continued, "but laughing nonstop is not as great as it seems."

The Bobos Babes thanked Barbara the Butterfly, hopped on Luke, and headed off.
Then all of a sudden, Princess Daphne made a hiccup followed by a cough.

They looked at each other and almost laughed, but they decided just to smile.
They had had enough laughter for one day ... well, enough laughter for a while.

CPSIA information can be obtained
at www.ICGtesting.com
Printed in the USA
BVHW022024040421
604096BV00003B/9